SPORTS JOKES

Compiled and Illustrated by
Viki Woodworth

Printed in the United States of America.

Distributed to Schools and Libraries
in the United States by
ENCYCLOPAEDIA BRITANNICA EDUCATIONAL CORP.
310 S. Michigan Avenue
Chicago, Illinois 60604

Library of Congress Cataloging-in-Publication Data
Rothaus, James.
Sports jokes / Jim Rothaus; compiled and illustrated by Viki Woodworth.
p. cm.
Summary: A collection of jokes about sports.
Example: Why do golfers take an extra pair of trousers with them?
In case they get a hole in one.
ISBN 0-89565-727-9
1. Wit and humor, Juvenile. 2. Sports–Juvenile humor.
[1. Sports–Wit and humor. 2. Jokes.]
I. Title. 91-17835
PN6371.5.R68 1991 CIP
818'.5402–dc20 AC

SPORTS JOKES

Compiled and Illustrated by

Viki Woodworth

THE CHILD'S WORLD

How many sides does a basketball have?
Two. The inside and the outside.

Where do tennis players sue each other?
In tennis court.

Confucius says: He who wants to bowl a perfect game has no time to spare.

What race starts with a tie?
A three-legged one.

What crime is committed in baseball?
Hit and run.

Why is it hard to drive a golf ball?
It doesn't have a steering wheel.

Why are referees and the Seven Dwarfs alike?
They both whistle while they work.

1st Horse: "Don't you know me?"
2nd Horse: "Your pace is familiar, but I don't recall your mane."

What is a gorgeous female boxer called?
A knockout.

Golf Instructor: Tee the ball.
Student: I see it, but why the baby talk?

Letter from football camp:
Dear Mom,
Please send food. All they serve here is breakfast, lunch and dinner.

How can you keep cool at a football game?
Stand next to a fan.

Why did the catcher carry a hammer?
To nail runners at the plate.

Where do you find a chicken at a base-ball game?
In fowl territory.

Why did they call for an ambulance at the ball park?
They needed a seventh inning stretcher.

Why did the Irishman, named O'Shea, love the football game?
Because at the beginning of the game everyone asked "O'Shea can you see?"

Track Coach: I have a new sprinter who is so fast he can turn the lights out in his room and be in bed before it's dark!

Dad: Stay away from tennis players.
Daughter: Why?
Dad: Because love means nothing to them.

What kind of running leads to walking?
Running out of gas.

Why did the athlete take his math homework to exercise class?
To reduce some fractions.

Why did the insecure football coach quit?
Everytime his team huddled he thought they were talking about him.

Why does a boxer take his gloves to bed?
To hit the sack.

What dogs are welcome at football games?
Hot dogs.

Coach: How does our center look for next week's big game?
Manager: He stops at a gas station and gets directions.

Why doesn't a basketball player take his ball with him on a trip?
So he's not penalized for traveling.

What has 22 legs and goes crunch, crunch, crunch?
A football team eating corn chips.

What is a baseball player's favorite sandwich?
A grand salami.

Dad: Son, in order to learn something you must start at the bottom.
Son: Dad, I want to learn to swim.

Why did the big game hunter give up hunting elephants?
The decoys were too heavy.

Where do divers eat their meals?
At pool tables.

Coach: How does your uniform fit?
Small Player: Great! Except the trousers are baggy around the armpits.

Sam: Did you hear the one about the high jump?
Tom: No.
Sam: I couldn't get over it.

How come it takes longer to go from second to third than from first to second?
Because between second and third there's a short stop.

Why do golfers take an extra pair of trousers with them?
In case they get a hole in one.

What does the catcher sing to his mitt?
Glove songs.

What color does a cheerleader like best?
Yeller.

When do frog baseball games start?
At the bug-inning.

What do golf socks look like?
They have 18 holes in them.

Why can't a bicycle stand up?
Because it's two-tired.

Why did the baseball player bring a screwdriver to the plate?
So he could hit a screwball.

How can you get out of a locked room with a baseball bat?
Strike three times and then you're out.

What do you have when there is no snow?
Rough sledding.

Why are umpires overweight?
They like to clean their plates!

Why did the rookie have coal on his face?
He'd just come up from the miners.

What do you call an escalator at a ball park?
A fan belt.

Why did the runner go to the veterinarian?
He had sore calves.

A baseball player is only as old as he fields.

Why did the boxer get fired from his job?
He punched the time clock.

What dog is most likely to win the heavy-weight title?
A boxer.

What kind of sportswear do frogs love?
Jumpsuits.

How tall should basketball players be?
Tall enough to have their ears pop when they sit down.

Which vegetable should never box?
Spinach–it can get creamed.

New Player: I'm a little stiff from running.
Coach: I don't care where you're from, just get out on that field and cover third.

What's a hermit?
A baseball mitt for girls.

What part of a uniform lasts the longest?
The underwear–it's never worn out.

Why did the bowling pins lie down?
They were on strike.

What do you get when you connect two bicycles?
Siamese Schwinns.

What moose is a great bowler?
Bowlwinkle.

Where does a jogger wash his shoes?
In running water.

What state sells the most football shirts?
New Jersey.

A cabbage, a hose and a tomato had a race. What happened?
Last time I looked: The cabbage was ahead, the hose was still running and the tomato was trying to ketchup.

Coach: Smith, go out there and get ferocious!
Smith: Ok coach, what's his number?

Why is a kangaroo a great baseball player?
It starts spring training at birth.

What do you call a 6′2″ basketball player?
Shrimp.

What kind of bear is a great swimmer?
A pool-ar bear.

What's a good way to meet people on the golf course?
Pick up the wrong ball.

Why is a leaking faucet like a horse race?
It's off and running.

What's the difference between a football player and a duck?
One is in a huddle, the other in a puddle.

What has four legs and catches flies?
Two outfielders.

How do Hawaiians play basketball?
With hula hoops.

What kind of dessert do basketball players hate?
Turnovers.

What do you get when you cross a basket-ball with a newborn snake?
A bouncing baby boa.

What candy should never wrestle?
A sucker. It always gets licked.

What do you say when two lawn mowers start a race?
On your mark–get set–mow!

Why should kids learn to bowl?
It gets them off the streets and into the alleys.

Have you ever seen a house fly?
No, but I've seen a home run.

What has 18 legs, red spots and catches flies?
A baseball team with measles.

What's another name for a baseball bat?
A fly swatter.

Why was Cinderella a crummy football player?
Because she had a pumpkin for a coach.

If a pig runs out into a baseball field and eats the ball that was just hit, what would it be?
An "in the pork" home run.

When did all the bases get stolen?
When the team took the field.

What do soccer players eat for breakfast?
Kix.

Why did the player on third base cry?
He wanted to go home.

What goes putt, putt, putt, putt, putt, putt, putt, putt?
A bad golfer.

Where do they serve soup to football players?
In the Soup-er Bowl.

What's Godzilla's best sport?
Squash.

What is the most famous golf match in American history?
The Boston Tee Party.

How did the glue run?
At a slow paste.

What does a baseball hitter love to hear?
Batter flattery.

When is a pitcher covered with ink?
When he's in the pen.

Why should you put a spider in the outfield?
It catches flies.

Why is a pitcher great on a camping trip?
He can pitch the tent.

Did King Arthur watch baseball?
Yes, at knight games.

Why did the jogger carry a fishing rod?
To catch her breath.

What's the difference between winning the NBA championship and having athlete's foot?
One is the thrill of victory; the other is the agony of "de feet."

Coach: Can you name five positions on a football team?
Student: Four tackles and a fullback.

Mother: It's time to get up, dear. It's twenty to eight.
Son: In whose favor.

Why are judges like basketball referees?
They both work the courts.

When does a coach look in a cookbook?
When he wants a better batter.

Where is a monster's favorite place to swim?
Lake Eerie.

What do baseball players wear in the snow?
Catcher's mittens.

Where should you keep your baseball mitt?
In the glove compartment.

Where do you hear tall tales about baseball?
In the bull pen.

Sally: Can we share your sled?
Sam: Sure, you can use it half the time!
Sally: Great!
Sam: I'll take it downhill and you can have it uphill!

What does a basketball player get when he has a personal foul?
A turkey of his very own.

What are a boxers favorite colors?
Black and blue.